llama llama red pajama

written and illustrated by
Anna Dewdney

VIKING

VIKING
Published by Penguin Group
Penguin Young Readers Group, 345 Hudson Street, New York, New York 10014, U.S.A.
Penguin Group (Canada), 90 Eglinton Avenue East, Suite 700, Toronto, Ontario, Canada M4P 2Y3
(a division of Pearson Penguin Canada Inc.)
Penguin Books Ltd, 80 Strand, London WC2R 0RL, England
Penguin Ireland, 25 St Stephen's Green, Dublin 2, Ireland (a division of Penguin Books Ltd)
Penguin Group (Australia), 250 Camberwell Road, Camberwell, Victoria 3124, Australia
(a division of Pearson Australia Group Pty Ltd)
Penguin Books India Pvt Ltd, 11 Community Centre, Panchsheel Park, New Delhi – 110 017, India
Penguin Group (NZ), 67 Apollo Drive, Rosedale, Auckland 0632, New Zealand
(a division of Pearson New Zealand Ltd.)
Penguin Books (South Africa) (Pty) Ltd, 24 Sturdee Avenue, Rosebank, Johannesburg 2196, South Africa

Penguin Books Ltd, Registered Offices: 80 Strand, London WC2R 0RL, England

First published in 2005 by Viking, a division of Penguin Young Readers Group
This special edition published in 2011 by Viking, a division of Penguin Young Readers Group

1 3 5 7 9 10 8 6 4 2

THE LIBRARY OF CONGRESS HAS CATALOGED THE ORIGINAL EDITION AS FOLLOWS:
Dewdney, Anna.
Llama llama red pajama / by Anna Dewdney.
p. cm.
Summary: At bedtime, a little llama worries after his mother puts him to bed and goes downstairs.
ISBN 978-0-670-05983-6 (hardcover)
[1. Mother and child—Fiction. 2. Bedtime—Fiction. 3. Llamas—Fiction. 4. Stories in rhyme.] I. Title.
PZ8.3.D498Ll 2005
[E]—dc22
2004025149

This edition ISBN 978-0-670-01420-0

Manufactured in China   Set in Quorum

For my own little llamas,

with thanks to Tracy, Denise, and Deborah.

Llama llama
red pajama
reads a story
with his mama.

Mama kisses
baby's hair.
Mama Llama
goes downstairs.

Llama llama
red pajama
feels **alone**
without his mama.

Baby Llama wants a drink.

Mama's at the kitchen sink.

Llama llama
red pajama
calls down to
his llama mama.

Mama says
she'll be up soon.

Baby Llama
hums a tune.

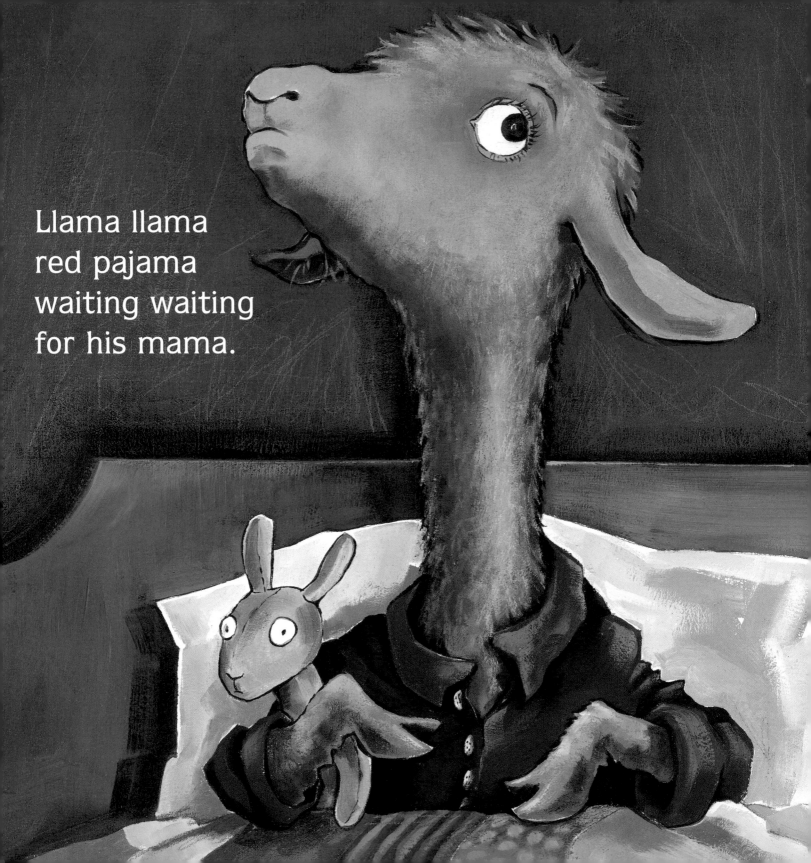

Llama llama
red pajama
waiting waiting
for his mama.

Mama isn't
coming yet.
Baby Llama
starts to **fret.**

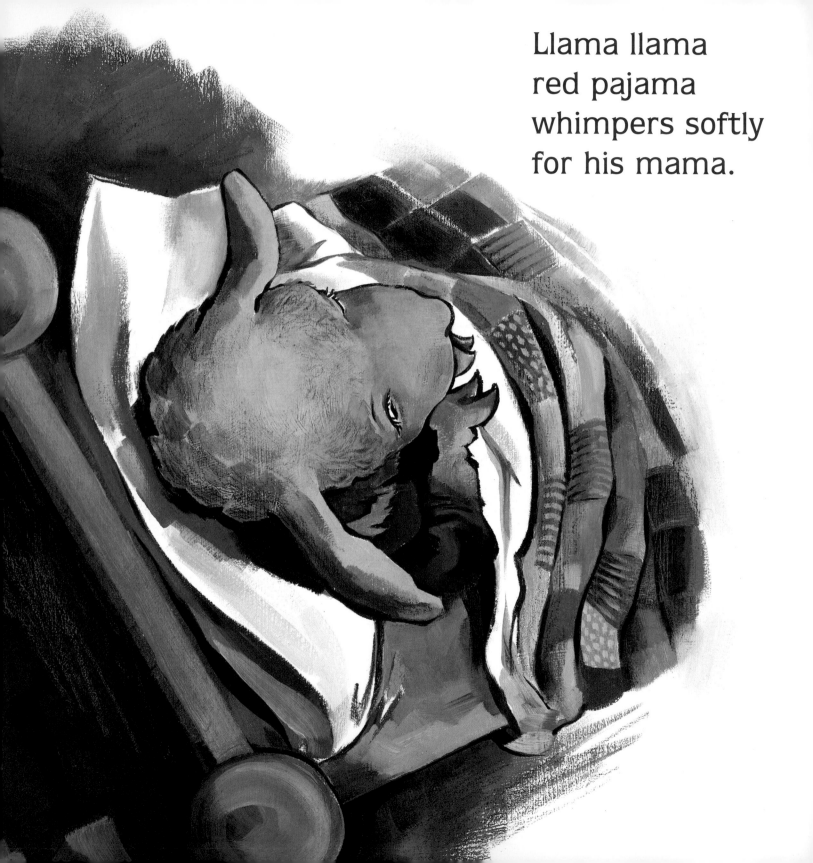

Llama llama
red pajama
whimpers softly
for his mama.

Mama Llama
hears the phone.

Baby Llama
starts to **moan**. . . .

Llama llama
red pajama
listens, quiet,
for his mama.

What is Mama Llama doing?

Baby Llama
starts **boo hoo-ing.**

Llama llama
red pajama
hollers loudly
for his mama.

Baby Llama
stomps and **pouts.**

Baby Llama
jumps and **shouts.**

Llama llama
red pajama
in the dark
without his mama.
Eyes wide open,
covers drawn . . .
What if Mama Llama's **GONE?**

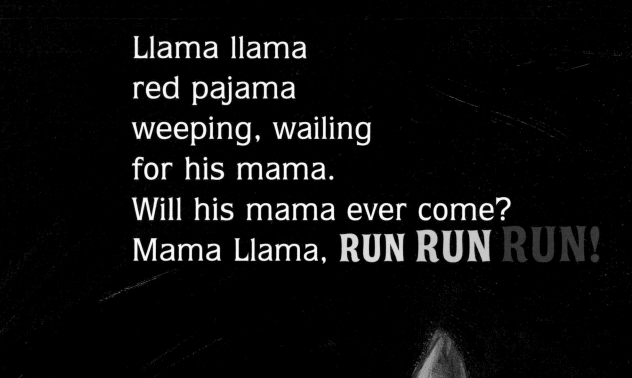

Llama llama
red pajama
weeping, wailing
for his mama.
Will his mama ever come?
Mama Llama, **RUN RUN RUN!**

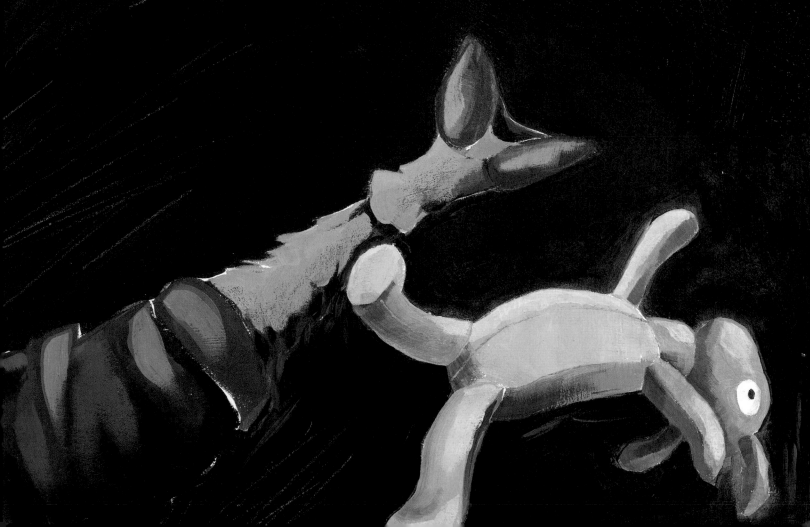

Baby Llama,
what a **tizzy!**
Sometimes Mama's
very busy.

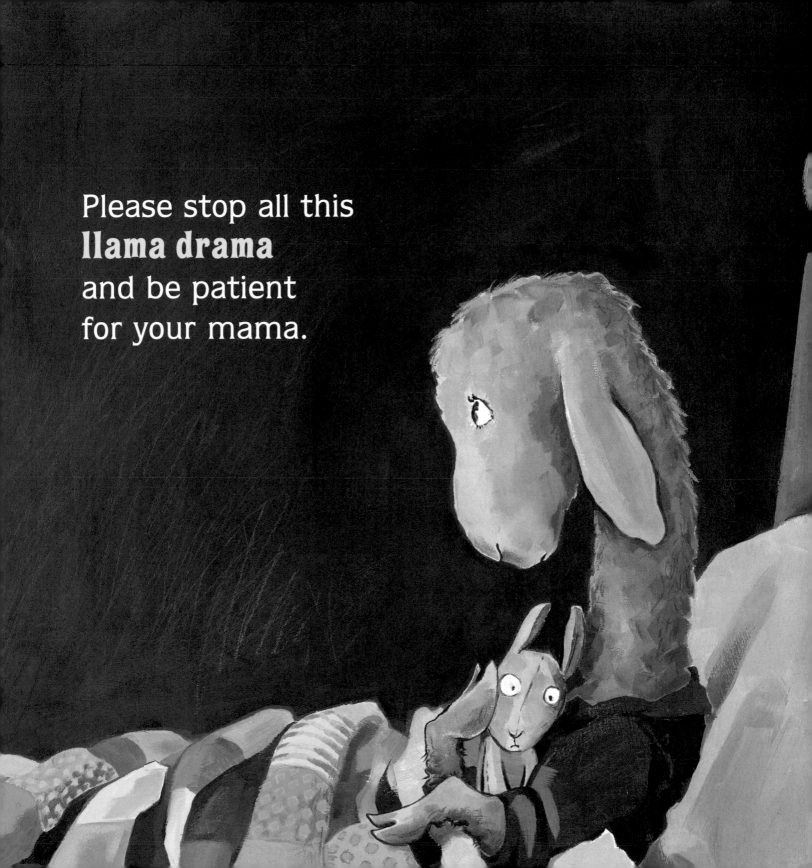

Please stop all this
llama drama
and be patient
for your mama.

Little Llama,
don't you know,
Mama Llama
loves you so?

Mama Llama's
always near,
even if she's
not right **here.**

Llama llama
red pajama
gets two kisses
from his mama,
snuggles pillow
soft and deep . . .

Baby Llama
goes to **sleep.**